HER FAULT

NJ Stallard

ꝐꝐ
PARTUS PRESS
Oxford · Reykjavík
MMXXII

Her Fault

CONTENTS

The Barbara Hepworth Blues	9
Total Eclipse	12
Negative Painting Exercise	13
Her Fault	14
Glass Cockerel	15
Bark	16
Carry-On	17
Red Umbrella	18
Boat Party	19
Ex	21

THE BARBARA HEPWORTH BLUES

At the bottom of the garden, my mother and a woman
dressed like Barbara Hepworth argue over a sculpture of
  my birth—

whether the bronze plinth is necessary,
the right shade of blue for the umbilical cord.

Hepworth adds a curl of hair with a toothbrush,
pats down its sides like a pony.

My mother sticks her chisel in, disappointed
by the arrangement of her legs, if she had her way

the sculpture would include a dancing fountain and hum
like a refrigerator filled with roses, sundials and a coat of arms,

her snacks, soft drinks and wine. Instead the sculpture stands
in the April shadows of overgrown gorse, a bundle

of cold clay, one arm in the air like the chimney
of the defunct engine house where my father

worked in the summer of '85, where copper wires crawled in
beneath the sea—no messages.

But what about the father? Hepworth asks.
Oh, he wasn't involved, my mother says.

Hepworth rolls her eyes, the whites of her eyeballs
like a cliff face, the grey of her overalls

like a gun. She begins to sing:
Don't turn your back on me, baby.

Blues like the sulky one in a rainbow.
Blues like your favourite moon.

With so many conflicting opinions, a therapist
had warned the sculpture of my birth of this moment

and offered some advice: be lucid.
Talk to the older generations as if talking to the sea.

Keep a list of all their errors, like those lists
you'll keep of all the things you eat while falling in love:

roast beef, feta cheese, champagne bonbons,
french fries, a blade of grass.

Keep a list of the places where you'll no longer have to be a sculpture
of a birth: the back seat of a minibus across Anatolia,

the heart-shaped swimming pool of Le Club Militaire.
Even Hepworth cannot capture the light as it falls

across your face on a Red Sea bottomless boat,
your feet pressed against the window of passing coral.

Isn't blue a bit obvious? What about yellow?
my mother interrupts. The woman who refused a pedicure

on her wedding day, who said if she wanted her toenails
a different colour she'd slam them in the car door.

Blues like the indoors with the outside coming at you with a
 chisel.
Blues like your favourite ocean.

Hepworth sighs and dusts her overalls, abandons the sculpture,
heads back up the garden path.

In the evening distance, yellow gorse rattles against
the windows of a passing train.

TOTAL ECLIPSE

Confronted by my loneliness, I throw myself into art and money.
I buy half a gallon of milk, far more than I need.

I am new here and I cannot control the sizes
or the destiny of bovine animals.

Yesterday I decided I did not like the country
and then I decided I did. Both positions are defensive.

There are conflicting opinions about milk, of course,
but either way the planet will not survive.

Sometimes the idea of meeting up is better than meeting up.
And so we have never met.

Most of my favourite poems feel like a bucket being
emptied out, but not tonight.

Tonight I am writing a poem about an eclipse
I have not seen.

I am not able to believe in the sun or mud
or that I am doing enough.

I am not admitting certain things
because I do not know how to describe them.

I let 'lonely' fill the gaps.

NEGATIVE PAINTING EXERCISE

Every detail is important.
For example, the oak tree outside the window

which had bare branches all winter
has grinning green leaves again.

Words continue to slip and slide
but not the ones I intended.

The windows are well positioned, you see,
and those greedy leaves block the view.

I can no longer see the grass on the hills
or the clouds scraped on like oil paint

against the blue-curtained sky.
Only my desk and its pile of pistachio shells.

HER FAULT

The gloomy city suddenly makes sense.
It's the earthquakes.
Memories of tremors handed down the generations
like wedding dresses or varicose veins.

No longer feeling so estranged,
she nails down the furniture,
straps down the white goods
and leaves a packed suitcase
by the door.

At night she listens for movement in the plates.
Not an 8 or 9, of course, but maybe 3.2 would do.
A smallish tremor.
A book falling off its shelf, or an alarmed cat.
Something to write home about.

GLASS COCKEREL

The cockerel sits on a mantelpiece—
ruby glazed beak, yellow breast,
smoky blue feathers,
blown freehand in Murano.

I remember that cockerel, wrapped
in the *Brighouse Echo* and laid to rest
in a shoebox, a paltry grave,
as we emptied the house.

A reminder of when colours stretched
outwards, collected grime,
before afternoons became
a chance to leave myself behind.

Days when the cockerel's
boiled-sweet rainbow
lit up the damp squalid room.
Chewed up cassettes,

a broken word processor.
Condensation collected
in jewelled gutters, blurring
the view of next door's patio.

BARK

One day she'll tend to this entire region,
planting trees and rare botanical breeds
and studying the soil in solitude.
No longer wandering like some dog
let out of the car for exercise,
wagging her tail at every stranger.

Years will be spent in solemn
scholarship, pruning the heads
of leopard-print gardenia.
Discovered by chance in her early 60s,
she'll handle her new fame with grace,
desiring no more than crisp pinafores
and quiet anonymity.

In good humour she'll look back on
the wasted years: all somersaults
and shortcuts. Days when it took
only half a *kinda, ok, fine.*
Half a man to ask and half a woman
to answer in her fluent: *sure.*
New leaves grow from old wood,
she'll quip, accepting her awards.

And the day she dies, we'll stuff
and mount her, hunched over a desk
in her best garden gloves,
examining the bark of a frankincense tree
and its pure white resin,
oozing like a wound.

CARRY-ON

You will need a certified copy of the death certificate. Speak to the airline operator in advance to check policies for travelling with cremated human ashes. To allow for screening, carry the remains in a non-metallic urn.

Expect to take it on as hand luggage. Expect to stand in line, unable to consolidate the idea of the man in the urn with the man who once sucked lime juice off his hangnails and explained the true beauty of the past participle.

The man who bought a blender for your new apartment and sprayed sangria up the walls.

The day the verb to swell became your eyes, to break became your plate, to drink became your punch.

Expect each word to refuse (refused, refusing?) to get in line.

Here they are: stiff and trying.

RED UMBRELLA

I bought it in Damascus
from a man who smelled
like Sunday afternoons
like Baba's cigars.
He said it was about to rain
and then it rained
and then it rained.

BOAT PARTY

What myth is this? the river blurts
and shudders through yet another
century, a brown thread unspooling from the Aegean's
mouth to the teeth of the Black Sea.

Except this river is not
a river, it's a strait.
The strait where Genoese soldiers once slept upright
in chilled stone forts.
The strait where star-spangled bishops still commit
a yearly crucifix,
chucked into salty depths and fetched
out by pilgrims
among the braindead, hormone-hard trout.

The strait where Io, transformed into a cow
and condemned to wander Earth,
swam from bank to bank
to escape the gadflies.

Flies regather now, era-less and inky faced.
Kiss beer bottles, dance in right angles
above the sunbathing bodies
of a boat party
where foreign correspondents
take their first day off in months.

Straight men, baseball-capped, clap their hands
as a tsarina in capri pants
sings the GI Blues.
The blonde reporter, who once bit
a man's face in Baghdad,

clutches her Tom Collins
and toasts to Io, the old cow,
who gave this strait its name.

The water grows apprehensive.
A girl in a red bikini
stands on the deck's edge
too scared to jump
through the thicket of flies.
She shrieks when she's pushed,
feels history bleeding into history.

Gadflies gather and whisper—
Io never shrieked.
What myth is this? the strait blurts
and shudders.
Waiting for the century,
or at least the day, to end.

EX

Oh, how I adore these failing
circumstances,
this hotbox of emotional uncertainty
as we, poised on sun loungers,
watch bare-chested militiamen
dive beyond the rocks.
The chef blows hot coals
with a hairdryer. There are brown
spots on the fronds. The weather is
savoury and kind.

Yes, let's admire the lines of my
phantom halterneck.
There were years I cared but
other years I tanned.
Car horn. The light slap of flip-flops
across the restaurant floor. The rainbow-painted
Ferris wheel of Luna Park, which
kept turning through the war.

Yes, let's take the sunbathers
to the Hague.
These are not my stories.
I don't want them anymore—
pressed against my teeth,
the wicked, prickled bubbles
of a burnt tongue.

Her Fault © NJ Stallard, 2022.

First published in Great Britain
in 2022 by Partus Press Ltd.
266 Banbury Road, Oxford OX2 7DL
www.partus.press

The right of NJ Stallard to be identified
as the author of this work has been
asserted in accordance with the
Copyright, Designs and Patents Act
of 1988. All rights reserved.

A CIP catalogue record for this book
is available from the British Library,
ISBN 9781913196066.

Designed and set by Studio Lamont.